Dear Parents:

Congratulations! Your child is taking the first steps on an exciting journey. The destination? Independent reading!

STEP INTO READING® will help your child get there. The program offers five steps to reading success. Each step includes fun stories and colorful art or photographs. In addition to original fiction and books with favorite characters, there are Step into Reading Non-Fiction Readers, Phonics Readers and Boxed Sets, Sticker Readers, and Comic Readers—a complete literacy program with something to interest every child.

Learning to Read, Step by Step!

Ready to Read   Preschool–Kindergarten
• big type and easy words • rhyme and rhythm • picture clues
For children who know the alphabet and are eager to begin reading.

Reading with Help   Preschool–Grade 1
• basic vocabulary • short sentences • simple stories
For children who recognize familiar words and sound out new words with help.

Reading on Your Own   Grades 1–3
• engaging characters • easy-to-follow plots • popular topics
For children who are ready to read on their own.

Reading Paragraphs   Grades 2–3
• challenging vocabulary • short paragraphs • exciting stories
For newly independent readers who read simple sentences with confidence.

Ready for Chapters   Grades 2–4
• chapters • longer paragraphs • full-color art
For children who want to take the plunge into chapter books but still like colorful pictures.

STEP INTO READING® is designed to give every child a successful reading experience. The grade levels are only guides; children will progress through the steps at their own speed, developing confidence in their reading.

Remember, a lifetime love of reading starts with a single step!

All rights reserved. Published in the United States by Random House Children's Books, a division of Penguin Random House LLC, New York.

Step into Reading, Random House, and the Random House colophon are registered trademarks of Penguin Random House LLC.

Visit us on the Web!
StepIntoReading.com
rhcbooks.com

Educators and librarians, for a variety of teaching tools, visit us at RHTeachersLibrarians.com

Library of Congress Cataloging-in-Publication Data is available upon request.

ISBN 978-0-593-17785-3 (trade) — ISBN 978-0-593-17786-0 (lib. bdg.) —
ISBN 978-0-593-17788-4 (hardcover) — ISBN 978-0-593-17787-7 (ebook)

Printed in the United States of America
10 9 8 7 6 5 4 3 2 1

Rocket
and the
Perfect Pumpkin

Pictures based on the art by Tad Hills

Random House 🏠 New York

It is fall!

"Do you want to find
a pumpkin with me,
Rocket?" Bella asks.

"Yes!" Rocket says.
"Today is the perfect day
to find a pumpkin!"

Rocket and Bella
go up the hill
to the pumpkin patch.

The pumpkin patch
is full of pumpkins!

Some are big.

Some are small.

Some have bumps.

Some have spots.

There are so many
shapes and sizes!

Rocket sees a pumpkin
he likes.
It is big, round,
and very orange.

"It is the perfect pumpkin!"
says Bella.

The pumpkin is
too heavy to carry!

Rocket and Bella
push and push.

The pumpkin starts
to roll.

They push and push.
The pumpkin rolls faster.

"Oh, no!" says Rocket.

The pumpkin
is getting away.

Rocket and Bella run
down, down, down
the hill.

The pumpkin rolls down, down, down the hill.

The pumpkin
bumps into
Mr. Barker's house.

Mr. Barker wakes up.

Mr. Barker is not happy.

Bark! Bark! Bark!

He sniffs the pumpkin.
It is big, round,
and very orange.

Rocket and Bella reach
Mr. Barker's house.
"Sorry!" Bella says.
"Our pumpkin got away."

"That is a perfect pumpkin!"
Mr. Barker says.

"You may have it!"
says Bella.

"Yes, it is for you!"
Rocket agrees.

Mr. Barker loves
his pumpkin.
He is very happy.

"Making friends happy feels even better than having a perfect pumpkin," says Rocket.

"Yes," Bella says.
"Making friends happy
feels great indeed."